FILTHY SEX TALES

EXPLICIT DIRTY EROTICA SHORT STORIES

KENNA DIVENS,CHARA GLADEY,STERLING KLEMM,FAE DEROSE,BREANA KHOR,CARRICE MCKELVY,MELISA POCHE,BLANCA CRANSTON,CANDRA AUBREY, PARKER HEIMANN

plicit Press

CHAPTER 1

A MAN KNOWS HIS EROTIC SENSATIONS

A MAN CAN ALWAYS TELL when a woman wants something from him. In this case, I knew that my girlfriend Lucy wanted something. She welcomed me home with a passionate kiss. If I wasn't certain before, I was sure now; Lucy wanted something. The fact that there was no hesitation on her part and the way she submissively obeyed my instructions was the biggest clue that she had an ulterior motive.

I took a deep breath as she took my dick in her hand and then into her mouth. Her mouth covered my dick perfectly as her tongue stroked my raw flesh. The warm wet feel of her tongue and mouth on my cock was enough to drive me near the point of insanity.

"Oh God, Lucy," I groaned, cocking my head back and letting out a long deep breath. This was the sweetest most amazing feeling ever; I could feel my juices running through my body, making their way down to my erect dick.

Her tongue lavished my cock, and she began moving her head rhythmically up and down my shaft. My fingers knotted in her hair as I held her in position and forced her head back and forth onto my cock. I could hear her gagging as I began thrusting my long dick into her mouth. With every hard thrust, the tip of my cock made contact with the back of her throat and she would try to pull away but I held on to her. If she was going to try to pull a fast one on me, then she'd better be prepared for what I had to dish out.

As my pleasure increased, I found it harder and harder to control my shaky legs. I eased off on Lucy, slowly releasing the portion of her hair that I had been pulling.

Now that I had allowed her total control, it seemed like she was out to get me to climax without any vaginal penetration. Her sucking was hard and vicious and she made slurping noises as she served me with a series of quick long sucks. I panted loudly as she flicked her hungry tongue repeatedly over and around the head of my cock.

"Now be quiet," she instructed, gripping firmly onto my dick with her hand. She focused all her attention on the head of my cock: Flicking her tongue over it, kissing it lightly, and then sucking it. She moaned as her tongue caressed almost every inch of the head of my cock. She was like an expert at work. Each move was carefully calculated and resulted in maximum pleasure. My dick got harder and harder as she worked her magic. My Gosh...if I were to continue letting her suck the head of my dick the way she was doing it, I would come in less than five minutes. But - NO. I wanted to get a little pussy action before ejaculating, and so I pulled away.

Lucy had a disappointed look on her face. "That coy little she-devil," I thought to myself, "She must have wanted me to cum in her mouth."

"Stand up and bend over here," I pointed to the small stool that she kept in the corner of the shower.

Propping her hands down on the stool, she bent over

and popped her ass out, facing me. "Nice..." I licked my lips as the palm of my hand made contact with her bare bum, in a loud

smack.

"OH!" She shrieked.

I slid my forefinger into the slit of her pussy; it was hot and wet, just the way I liked. She moaned as I slipped another two fingers into her moist core. "You like that, don't you?"

"Uh-huh," she whispered.

"Uh-huh is not an answer. Say YES!" I ordered firmly, jabbing my fingers deeper into her pussy, causing her to let out a cry.

"YES! YES! YES!"

"Good girl," I removed my fingers from her moistness and stroked her tender flesh. Lucy moaned - her voice laced with pleasure. She was enjoying this.

"I know you're up to something, my love. No good I assume. Now tell me, what is it?" "I...I...I don't...don't know what you... *Mean*!" she struggled to let her words out. I had now

bent over and was darting my tongue into her pussy. She tasted so good; her juices seemed to coat my tongue.

Parting her legs further, I tilted my head a little to the side and stroked her moist tender flesh with my hungry tongue. Her legs were shaking and the shower was filled with the sound of her moaning in ecstasy. Over and over I pleasured her with my tongue, licking her pussy lips, slowly at first then sucking their juicy flesh. Gliding my tongue upwards, I found her swollen bud.

"OH God!" she moaned out, as I captured her clitoris with my mouth, sucking and tugging on it lightly at first, increasing my suction as I went along. The more I sucked her clit, the more I realized how much she was trying to wiggle away from my desire-filled mouth.

"Bring that ass back here!" I grabbed onto her ass and forced her in place. Darting my tongue viciously into her pussy, licking and sucking all her juices.

"Ohhhh...." She cried out, bucking her wet pussy against my lips.

I didn't stop there; I re-introduced my fingers and worked the insides of her wet juicy cunt.

Fucking her over and over with my fingers, while sucking her clitoris.

"OH God...Yes...Yes. YES!!!" She cried out letting out a little groan at the end of it all. Her juices flowed freely onto my waiting tongue as she summited her climax.

I didn't give her even a minute to catch her breath. Within that moment I plunged my dick into her wetness without warning.

Another loud shriek escaped her lips as I began moving in and out of her temple of delight.

Her pussy was warm and inviting and her juices flowed out onto my dick like honey. It was amazing; I served her with a series of long hard thrusts, followed by quicker shorter thrusts. Although I tried hard to control my climax, her sweetness was irresistible. I pulled out immediately when I realized that I was about to cum.

"Why? Don't stop now," it was then that I noticed that she too was about to come yet again. "Don't worry, I've got something even better," I assured her.

"Fuck...Jesus Christ!" she exclaimed, as my tongue, traced the hole of her anus. I was not an ass man, but however today, I went with the mood. Right now, the mood seemed to call for some anal, torture!

"Jason, you know...OH GOD!" she moaned again, as I

stuck my tongue into her anus. "Uh...." she moaned some more, as I continued to thrust my tongue into her anus, sucking

and licking the hole as I went along.

She could barely speak; I managed to shut her up and everything. Any attempt at the resistance that she had was completely forgotten.

Finally, I moved on to the second part of my anal invasion. Now that I had pleasured her, and she was more willing to participate in my anal explorations, I needed to feel her tight anus hugging against my long dick.

Pulling my face away from her bum, I parted her ass cheeks with both hands, and slowly brought my dick to her back entrance. I swabbed my cock with saliva for extra lubrication and placed it at the tip, ready to plunge deep down into her anus.

"Please don't do it too hard," she begged, realizing my intentions.

"Now, listen to me," I yanked her by her hair, hoisting her body upwards. "You don't tell me what *I will* and *will not* do, okay!" I released her, with much more force than was needed. With my stern warning, I penetrated her anus with a hard thrust.

Her cry echoed throughout the bathroom, and I thanked God that we lived in a detached house. "Shut up! Shut the *fuck up!*" I ordered, and then buried my dick into her ass once more.

She cried out some more as I penetrated her again. I loved it when she would try to muffle her cries. It was not that I hated hearing her in her ecstasy; it was just that it seemed like a little more fun when she tried to control it. I slowly pulled my dick from her anus, and just when she was getting comfortable, I rammed my cock even deeper into her.

A loud shriek escaped her lips. Her anus was so tight, its muscles seemed to be contracting and trying to resist the entry of my cock. Her tightness on my cock was literally driving me insane, and as I continued to thrust my dick into her anus, I found it harder and harder to control myself. Finally, I let loose and increased the momentum of my thrusts. My body slammed against her ass with every thrust, sending ripples through her ass cheeks, and shockwaves through my entire body. I let out several loud groans, while she let out moans of pleasure. Her cries had changed from cries of pain, to cries of pleasure.

Finally, with a mighty hard thrust, I buried the full length of my dick, deep down into her anus. At that very moment, a loud groan escaped my lips as I reached my earth-shattering climax, exploding a load of my hot liquid into her anus. She too let out a loud moan as she also summited her climax.

It took us a moment to calm down and the fact that we were already in the shower made it a lot easier.

I stepped out of the shower and my eyes, caught sight of Lucy sitting at the edge of the bed waiting for me.

"Sit with me," she encouraged, lightly tapping the spot directly next to her. And here it was, I knew it was coming. The favor that she needed.

CHAPTER 2

CUNT, COPY AND PASTE

I HAD JUST STARTED my new job at a very ritzy downtown office and I was excited about going back to work this week. This office wasn't your typical office setting. Everyone seemed to be a bit kinky. I thought I was imagining it at first until the day I walked into the ladies' room and could hear two girls going after each other's pussies like starved tigers. It got me so wet that I went into the stall hiked one leg up onto the stool and looked down at my furry pussy while I started to stroke her throbbing button.

Before I was done I was literally slapping my clit to pink and throbbing pulsations. I moaned some before I realized that the two chics in the next stall probably heard me. I was momentarily embarrassed but then I heard them gushing all over each other and it made me cum one more time. It was like the three of us all came at once. What was really erotic is that when the three of us emerged we simply chatted and had a little small talk while we rinsed the pussy scents from our fingers and mouths. We kind of smiled with a look full well knowing that we had all just been very nasty girls and we loved it. As the blonde walked past me to the door, I could still smell a lingering aroma of hot cunt waft through the air.

I made my way to my desk and opened my legs to the geek sitting at the desk beside me. I wasn't wearing any panties and I knew he could see my still dripping hard worked over snatch smiling at him. He cleared his throat pushed his glasses up to his nose and scooted as far as he could under his desk. I imagine he was hiding a raging boner underneath that desk. It wasn't long before he scurried to the man's bathroom no doubt to rub one out. I giggled playfully, gave my clit a loving slap, and pulled my skirt down. Gosh, I loved my job!

I actually did a few hours of honest work before I headed to the copy machine down at the end of the hallway. I walked into the copy room and there I saw the office stud-muffin making copies of some paperwork. I smiled seductively at him and he gave me a gorgeous smile back. I sat down in a chair and did the Sharon stone leg cross and uncross for him. At first, he seemed to not even notice, but on my last go-around, he looked from his peripheral vision over at me and just in time to see my gaping hairy cunt. I saw him do a quick look at his crotch. He was obviously worried he had a bulging woody chewing its way out of his work slacks.

He walked over to me and gave me a brief kiss and asked me to meet him in his office for lunch together. I told him a sure thing and shook my hot ass all the way back to my office. I could feel him looking at me as I walked away. I always loved it when a man did that. He made me feel like a complete woman from head to toe. I went and did a bit more work before I heard the lunch bell. I powdered my nose and added some hot pink lipstick and headed down the hall to his office. He quickly waved me inside and told me to lock the door behind me.

I was in the process of locking the door and he came up behind me and grabbed my throbbing tits from my sheer mauve blouse. He rolled my nipples between his thumb and index finger, making my buds stand out like 2 pointed cones. After he twirled my horny nips a few times I felt an immense wetness fill my greedy pussy. I got so horny I was practically begging for him to screw me to the wall. He lifted my skirt above my jiggling ass and slid his swollen pole deep inside my chambers. I groaned in half pain and half pleasure. He sucked and bit my neck from behind me as he screwed me like a beast. He gave it to me like I wanted and he gave it to me hard and fast. It seemed like only a minute but when we heard the bell we realized we had been screwing like animals for 30 minutes. He released his seed in me as I thrust back onto him and slammed down to his balls and creamed over his shaft. My cunt formed a chokehold around his girth and it popped out with a suction sound when he pulled back out of me. If I had it my way, this cock and I would fuck the rest of the afternoon non-stop but it wasn't possible. I needed to get back to work and he did too. I pulled my skirt down and wiped the cum off that was dripping down my leg and I walked silently out the door. On my way out I damn near ran smack dab into the geek that had his desk beside me. "Oops!" I said as my pointed tits grazed his chest. I also felt a pretty massive boner forming in his slacks. I wondered if maybe he had been listening to me and the hot guy fucking. My guess was he had and he loved it.

I went about my secretarial chores for the rest of the day feeling very satisfied and a bit sore from the pounding I had taken from the 9-inch cock I had screwed earlier. He had done me hard and done me good and satisfied me as well. I was the last one leaving the office that day and a good idea hit me. I saw the lonely Xerox copy machine humming sadly down the corridor. It almost sounded like some distant lonely cat in need of a good stroke. So I made my way down to the end of the hallway chuckling to myself all the way. Boy was I a genius or what!

I walked sexily towards the groaning white copier. I flipped the silver switch on the machine and hiked my skirt up. I made sure there was plenty of paper in it. I hopped up on top of the copy machine and spread my pussy lips open wide. She smiled beautifully for her portrait I must say. I made about 10 different copies of it to place in various offices. I carefully selected the horny men and women I wanted to see my smiling pussy on Tuesday morning as they sipped their morning Java. I wondered how many would choke on their first few sips. The best part was as they looked at it, the mystery of whose pussy it was would always remain. I never had any intention of letting the cat out of the bag. My lips were fucked, copied, and pasted shut.

CHAPTER 3

FEMALE GLORYHOLE SEX

THE BOYS and I from the construction site ate lunch at Hooters. We had a great time and I met this girl named Anna-Ludken. I got her phone number and planned to call her when I got back to the office. I run the construction site. I'm the office manager. We stopped at a gas station we always bypass. I guess I had too many beers because I had to use the bathroom. "Let's stop here boys. Go in and get some lottery tickets. One day we're all going to quit, rich!"

As I neared the small dingy bathroom, I noticed a hot-looking raven-haired beauty with short hair and a pink metallic bow around her chest for a blouse. She also wore a pink miniskirt decked out in ruffles around the hem and black converse gym shoes. I nodded to her as she caught my eye in that sexy outfit.

She smiled, and I noticed her flower-lined tattoo below her belly button.

. . .

I didn't think much of it. I had already planned on calling Anna-Ludken when I got back in my office. As I entered the one bathroom and locked the door behind me, I heard a soft voice saying, "Look here."

I looked around and saw a bowl size hole in the wall. I finished pissing and zipped up. I moved back from the urinal, squatted, and peeked inside the hole. All I saw was the pretty tanned color and a line of flowers. Then I understood. This was one of those gloryholes, only a glory hole for women.

I became intrigued.

"That's one pretty tattoo."

"I've got a prettier flower than those!" the soft voice replied.

I kept looking as the hole vacated and I saw directly into the women's bathroom.

"I'm the perfect gift for the perfect gift." She turned around three-hundred and sixty degrees. If I thought Anna-Ludken of Hooters was pretty, then this pink bow tie blouse girl was a knockout! She bent over and the ruffled hem of her hot pink skirt landed right over her asshole and framed her juicy wet-looking cunt. The girl bent lower and her cunt hole opened up. Her thick inner labia lips parted. I saw the best glory hole made on earth. Her pink pussy puckered tight, and thick and wet. This girl must be a virgin or a near virgin. I couldn't wait to get inside her.

· · ·

"Let's meet."

"We're meeting," she cooed.

"Put your tongue inside the bowl hole," she said cheerfully.

I did as Pink Bow Tie girl asked. All I could see was the wall with a phone number written over the hole. I waggled my tongue and soon heat neared. My nose smelled the taste of the sea.

Then, not to be outdone, my tongue tasted the slippery sea oil of her pussy.

"Gobble gobble," she ordered.

I licked her pussy juices up. She must have recently masturbated because up and down her silky folds of flesh, she was slippery as the bottom of a bowl of movie popcorn. I darted my lips out.

I pushed her flesh left and right. I even sucked her long inner lips, near her clit deep into my mouth.

"You eat pussy like a girl." "I'm all man!"

"I want to meet you."

"We're meeting," I fed her seductive line back to her. "Come around to the women's bathroom."

She said, and she turned around and pushed her dark

pubic hair closer to the bowl hole. I saw the flowers again and her clit simmering in her fuck oils.

"I can't stand it," she breathed hard. "I'm going to cum!"

"I am so horny now!" I replied and licked harder and faster. I cupped my tongue and lifted her thick clit upward and then swathed her clit left and right as fast I could. She pressed her groin closer to the bowl hole. Her lower belly practically had a little red ring around her Venus mound and clit.

"I'm coming! Don't stop whoever you are!"

I grabbed the wall. Realizing that was useless, I pulled my mouth back and squeezed my thick wrist through the bowl.

"Oh, you clever Dude!" She stepped back and allowed my eager fingers to dip into her pussy folds. I pinched her thick juicy clit. She pulled back. I took the hint and slipped my fingers lower into the curvature of her pelvic floor. My fingers flicked east and west, as I pushed into her sex further, and further. My index finger moved past her piss hole. I pulled back my fingers unable to resist. I licked them.

"Mmmmmmm."

.   .   .

"I taste good," she cooed.

"Mmmmm-hmmmm."

I stopped licking and sucking my fingers and stuck them back in the hole. I strained to see inside it. I made out the Pink Bow Tie girl had her legs spread wide. Just under the bottom of the hole, I made out her black converse gym shoes. "You must be eighteen years old."

"Stop talking and finger fuck me!"

I focused on pushing my fingers where my dick meat wanted to explore. I reached further inside until I felt her flesh open up. Her slick hole beckoned. I pushed one digit inside her hot cavern flesh.

She wiggled her hips. "Nice. Sweet."

"You're going to make me come, Mister."

I danced two of my fingers up her fuck sheath. "I'm almost full."

I managed to squeeze three fingers up her hot dripping snatch. "I can't take much more!"

I folded my fingers in on each other and forced four fingers inside her dewy fuck slot. "I'm coming! You nasty finger cunt fucker!"

Her body quivered around my pushing, and retreating fingers. "This feels good," I said, proud of myself.

She stiffened and a large flow of slippery girly goo dripped over my fingers. "Awwww. Uuuggggg. I'm squirting!" She cried. She pulled back suddenly. "What? Where are you Raven cutie?"

"Composing myself. Making myself presentable."

"I'm ready to meet you," I said anxiously. "My dick is hard as fuck."

She giggled. "Give me five minutes. Don't leave until I'm outside waiting for you!"

I waited five minutes in the stinking bathroom. Then I hurried out, walked to the door, and knocked. No one answered. So I bravely pushed in and no one was there. All the guys wondered what was taking me so long. When I got back in the van, they raved and talked about the hot little Pink Bow Tie girl who left the bathroom in a hurry. The Pink Bow Tie girl who flashed her bare pussy and got into a little black corvette with her equally pretty girlfriend and drove off.

Damn, I thought to myself. I should have left earlier and gotten her number. The boys laughed at my ups and downs in the dating department. I never did tell them what happen in that female glory hole. Some things should remain private between a man and his girl. Even if she is a fleeting girlfriend.

CHAPTER 4

FUCKING IN THE THIRD-DIMENSION

THE COMPUTER ANIMATION game said Bobsey was a single girl from Czechoslovakia with long platinum blonde hair, and blue eyes, and her fetish involved the shower and a webcam. Right away when I logged on, I expected to see some hot pretty pussy. I wasn't disappointed when I entered a huge room and on a long mauve couch sat this gorgeous creature, wearing tiny gold earrings, holding a remote in her hand. Bobsey wore a long dark blue opened jacket and nothing else. "I'm Bobsey," the seductive voice replied to my entry.

You don't expect a girl to greet you right away in these places. Usually, they wait for you to type something or say something. Her legs spread wide showing her pink gash, glistening in the bright lights. . I settled back and admired her boobs when the screen went black suddenly.

.   .   .

White words flashed across the screen. Bobsey went to take a shower. Meet her in the 3-D shower for $2.99. Two dollars and ninety-nine cents isn't much to see Bobsey dripping wet all over. So I paid the fee and went inside. Immediately based on my profile the computer gave me a body; black and strong looking, with a short afro and my personality was romantic. A bouquet of flowers of yellow, blues and pinks, and greens appeared in my hand. I was looking at myself in a mirror dressed in a white towel robe. I couldn't believe it! It seemed so real.

I walked closer and I heard the hot shower water running. I heard Bobsey chatting, talking. No, she was complaining about the lack of sex.

"I don't get to fuck men until I go home once a month."

"Someone will come in and fuck you soon, Bobsey, I assure you."

I pushed the door open and ended up inside the shower with Bobsey. Steam assaulted my nose. The fog made her white skin seem rosy pink. Her one hundred and nineteen pounds weight all registered to me!

"Hi," Bobsey said. She let her smile warm up my face. "You must want to fuck me in my favorite spot."

"If your favorite place is your pussy . . . that'd be me." I presented her with the flowers. She blushed and opened the shower door.

· · ·

It was surreal. I had a real body. Bobsey embraced me and her skin touched my skin. The emotions the 3-D character experienced registered through the computer console. I did know how they did it, at the bawdy house. I didn't care after Bobsey planted the slowest, tender French kiss on my eager lips, we hugged and we kissed some more.

I ran my hands through Bobsey's wet blonde hair. My hand slid down her back as I pushed her into my groin closer.

"Remove the robe, silly boy."

I removed my towel robe. Bobsey grabbed my dick in her tiny palm. She wore a lovely small ring on her wedding finger. Every time her gold fingernails moved my dick up and down in the water, washing my dick, I thought about marrying her. I slipped my finger under her flat butt cheeks and pressed my index finger into her cooze. The hot wetness invited me further inside her. I pushed another finger in until I had buried two digits up her bald box. Bobsey leaned on me and kept pumping my cock meat. She hooked her left calf around my right and pulled my face down to her puffy tit flesh.

I took a lick. I took a suck. I swallowed her areola and nipple all at once and hallowed my cheeks, bringing a delightful peal from her pretty lips. She closed her eyes and said, "Fuck me."

I pressed the turn her around the button. I pressed the forward button and Bobsey now faced the shower wall, as the warm water ran down her back and my chest. Her flat ass poked outward. Her pussy was clearly visible under her best buns on a webcam. I reached under and parted her pussy lips and licked my fingers. "You taste good and slippery."

"I hope you want to fuck all night."

I tried to keep separate her words from my obvious 3-D experience. If I fucked her all night, I'd be broke. However, fucking her for thirty minutes didn't seem so bad at $4 a minute.

"If you press the 'I love you' button, the price drops to $2 per minute.'"

Love made things easier. I pressed the 'I love you, Bobsey,'" button and my price dropped, doubling my time. I pulled her butt cheeks apart and mounted my mark. I pressed inside her succulent pussy snatch easy and slow. Her hotness engulfed my column of male attention. "You're so big," Bobsey started moaning and squirming her butt back against my hairy groin. "This is the best place to fuck."

How they made the tightness of Bobsey's grinding, bumping, humping, shaking pussy translate through the remote to my cranny hunter is beyond me. The wonders of discovery and mechanics. I pushed further inside Bobsey.

She raised her right leg on the side of the tub. I reached under and stroked her clit. Her clit tremors started my own dickhead to swell bigger than ever before. I lodged myself high up inside her pussy core. I didn't want to blast off. I held off fighting her wild sexy movements trying to send my semen into orbit upside the hallow universe of her womb. Finally, it was too much. The surge of scalding hot semen erupted from my pussy stopper and sent man milk all up her girly spaces.

I knew Bobsey had a good time because her skin flushed. She developed goosebumps and she squealed like a pig at orgasms. Of course, the shower made everything sound classy like a symphonic opera. I pulled out right before the time limit ran out. The computer screen went black and said, "Thanks for loving Bobsey. She hopes to see you again soon."

Three-Dimension fucking is new in the bawdy houses in Europe. The only thing missing was the smell of sweet Bobsey's wet pussy. Hopefully, if I love her one hundred more times, I'll get a free trip to sniff and lick Bobsey's sweet-musky snatch up close and personal.

CHAPTER 5

LAST FUCK, FIRST FUCK DATE

SUZY FINISHED ARGUING with her boyfriend for the last time. "No, absolutely not. I will not give you one last fuck for the road, Brad!"

Her boyfriend begged because Suzy was hot. Her figure oozed sex appeal. Her smiles said fuck all my holes. Her long straight blonde hair reminded him of one of the cheerleaders gone wild.

While Suzy knew her considerable charms, she didn't learn how to capitalize on them until one day at the movies. She went alone. She sat in a large theater converted into a place for showing art films. Films that usually had a good amount of sex, but not exactly a porn film. People didn't come in with raincoats or anything. They were college professors. Students of the theater or film schools nearby. And the occasional scout looking for a new actress or actor.

Suzy sat in the back and quickly noticed a man, tossing his head back. She casually looked again as a film scene revealing more light appeared. A woman in a flowery dress knelt on her knees between the man's legs. Her saucy face looked upward as her tongue licked the man's hard pecker like it was a lollipop. She then brought his thick live dildo forward and engulfed him again. She bobbed her red hair up and down quickly, and then she changed up to long slow strokes. She pulled up again and the man forced her head back down and fucked her face. He jerked his hips upward and the woman's cheeks hollowed in as another bright scene flashed across the large movie screen.

Suzy's pussy grew wet and she spread her legs. The woman's trembling hands reached up to the side of her mouth and wiped a trickle of white sperm from her mouth. She got up and adjusted her dress. After a few minutes, the man and woman left.

Suzy spread her legs watching the film. But her mind projected the woman in the flowery dress giving the blowjob on the big screen! Soon Suzy panted and closed her legs tighter around her hand buried deep inside her snatch. That's when the stranger showed up and sat next to her.

"I've seen this film before. He does a good job kissing, but I'm way better than that."

Suzy couldn't believe her ears. She removed her pussy-drenched hand, hesitant at his reaction. "I've never seen it. I like the acting."

"You should see the pie-eating scene."

Suzy gasped and then smiled. Was he serious, she mused?

"I'm serious. The pie-eating scene isn't special." He knelt down on his knees. "I'll relieve your tension and stress, Miss-_"

"Miss," Suzy replied. She wasn't about to divulge who she was when she didn't know who he was.

The nineteen-year-old man moved from the outside of Suzy's thighs to inside them. Suzy held her legs tightly together at first.

The man didn't move. He waited patiently like her crotch would spout water and quench his thirst in a second now.

Suzy raised her own flowery black and yellow skirt and parted her legs more. She smelled her own cunt scent waft and hit her nose.

The young man's fingers found the lace band of her white panties and tugged on them. Suzy knew what to do. She lifted up. He removed her panties and inhaled. "Nothing better than the smell of pussy melting."

"I'm melting for your tongue. Do it!" Suzy finally broke down and said. "I thought you'd never ask," he replied, hotly.

He slid both hands toward her heated core. His fingers pulled apart her thick pussy labials. Inside a generous lubrication of white cream waited in her fold flaps. The man dipped his head and tongue right into her girl sauce. He rocked his tongue up and down her groove. He was a pro. His nose grazed against her clit. His tongue flipped her inner and outer labia flaps. His tongue sent ripples of pleasure through her curvy cunt skin. He pushed two fingers into her cunt hole and twisted his fingers.

His maddening movements churned up another glob that slipped down the young man's throat. She heaved her chest up and grabbed her boobs with both hands. She bent her calves behind his back. Suzy pulled the man up higher by his elbows. She scooted down.

Now they were on the same playing field.

"Fuck me!" Suzy said. "I want to come to the theater!"

He rose higher and his cock slipped inside. His face was sloppy with her juices. Suzy entangled her fingers in his slick black hair. Her body froze as she came shaking and squeezing on his throbbing cock meat.

The young man kept fucking. He held his seed tight and hot in his ball sacks. His movements went slow and smooth. Suzy petting his hair. She ran her fingers through his groin.

Another man sat down beside her.

The stranger looked up from between Suzy's trembling legs. His face is glossy with her fuck oils. "This is my cousin, Jay."

Suzy panted, hard, "Hi—J—Jay!"

Jay immediately started to roll her tits under her pink blue and gray striped blouse. He rubbed her right tit using the front of his hand. When he withdrew his hand, he pinched Suzy's neglected left tit.

Suzy came!

Suzy slumped back into the theater chair. Things couldn't get any better, she thought. The theater went dark.

Jay said, "They are changing the reel. This happens with art films."

"A lot," said the stranger who refused to reveal his name. The stranger pulled Suzy off the red theater seat and turned her hip to face Jay. Jay already had his hot cock out stroking it. He was huge, Suzy noticed as she looked back over her shoulder in an erotic daze.

The stranger took the seat to the right of Suzy. As Suzy leaned forward, the stranger pushed his dripping cock toward Suzy's mouth.

She willingly opened her mouth as Jay willingly opened her fuck hotspot behind.

The two cousins worked up a nice rhythm. Pushing his cock into her wet mouth, watching his dong slide down her throat, the stranger sighed. He winked at his cousin. His cousin started fucking faster. He was fucking her smooth and slow at first.

Now he pulled on her inner cunt flap preventing the tissue from slipping inside her cunt as he fucked her. This made Suzy feel wildly different. Her pussy flap was wet. Jay massaged her cunt flap in his fingertips. While his dick moved inside Suzy, feeling tighter because of less lubrication. Suzy moved her ass lewdly higher and higher into the air to make Jay feel even bigger and tighter.

Suzy's eyes blurred over as she felt the stranger slip past her gag reflect. He froze. He let his cock soak inside her throat saliva juices like some turkey basting. His cock throbbed inside her, giving her another wonderful new sensation. Suzy swallowed around his cock. Her tongue moved up and down his fuck meat until the stranger spurted, three foamy loads down her throat.

He held onto her face, so some of his cum had no choice but to spill out the side of her cheeks.

Jay by this time held her hips and froze. He unloaded his man milk four times. Suzy actually felt his dick meat leaping inside her fuck slice. Suddenly all his sluicing juices ran out of her cunt and down her thighs.

. . .

The two men left Suzy like that bent over the theater chair in the back. Skirt over her thin hips. Her blouse pulled up over her tits. Cum trickling out both her mouths. Suzy caught her breath as the second half of the art film began. She took out a tissue and wiped up the excess of their love-making. She sniffed the pungent cloth, stuffed the thing back up her cunt, and went home satisfied at last.

CHAPTER 6

LIBRARY TRYSTS

THERE WAS a specified portion in our huge college library where there were no strict librarians on duty. This was called the "inner sanctum." It was here where some students petted, necked, and even copulated when they could no longer contain their sexual cravings.

I have never been to that portion of the library, simply because the boys in my class had never taken a second look at my plain face. Anyway, I think that most of them are jerks too, so it didn't bother me a lot - except for Al.

Al was not handsome, but he had a certain smile that I had loved so much. He did not join the rowdy boys in their notorious parties and nights out. He was also intelligent, and this was what attracted me most.

My raging hormones had made me masturbate every night, and during my self-induced orgasms, I had concocted a devious plan to entrap my lifetime love - Al.

That day, I wore my sassiest dress to school. I put on blue eye contact lenses to add some color to my plain looks.

Confident, I approached Al, after our first class. "Could I ask a favor?" I piped shyly.

"Sure," he looked surprised.

"Can you help me with the Quality Assurance computations?"

I pulled him to his feet, and led him near the "inner sanctum." He looked at me, reluctant to occupy the last table in the area.

I opened my notebook and sat close to him. He moved away discreetly. I was so horny that I forgot my shyness.

It was morning, and there were only two students, ten tables away from us. I was lucky. *Now is my chance,* I thought. I may never get that chance again.

Underneath the table, I slid the soles of my feet up and down against his legs and thighs. He jerked away, but I persisted and continued rubbing them with my own. When he did not move but had closed his eyes instead, I dropped one hand on his crotch and felt overjoyed that he had a beginning erection. Emboldened that I was able to arouse him, I caressed his penis beneath his pants.

He pretended to push my hand away, but his rugged breathing betrayed what he truly felt. He wanted me to go on.

My fingers fondled his growing manhood, massaging his shaft with a sliding motion, steadily but gently. I kept on with the mesmerizing movement until I saw his face become suffused with passion.

His hands shot down to my pussy as well. He inserted his fingers into my panties and started rubbing my already wet pussy. I heaved a lusty sigh and increased the rhythm of my finger's movement on his dick.

When he touched my clit, I bit down on my lower lip to stifle a cry of delight. He noticed my reaction and concentrated on my clit, flicking it relentlessly with his thumb and index finger. How he managed it with my undies on, was beyond me.

We continued to fondle and caress each other when two girls came into the area. They were coming our way. We stopped momentarily and pretended to be reading our notes, but our fingers went back to what they were doing; we just were not able to stop the careening train of lust that has started rolling.

Only the soles of our feet were visible under the table, so we continued pleasuring each other. We had to achieve orgasm. I felt then that I could let him fuck me on the table itself, and I would not care less. I was as horny as ever.

The two girls left after a few minutes, with just a glance in our direction. I was not able to hold on any longer. The students a few tables away were busy too, perhaps with their own sexual escapades.

I pushed Al into the cubicle of the huge bookshelves and frantically pulled his pants halfway to his knees. We bumped into the sturdy bookshelf as he hiked my skirt and slid down my panties to my thighs. We were kissing passionately, suckling at each other's tongue and lips. His hand was fumbling with his tumescent penis as he rammed it into my moist vagina.

I lifted my right leg and wrapped it around his waist as he cupped my buttocks so he could thrust his eager dick deeply into my waiting pussy. It felt so good, I bit his lower lip gently as the amazing pleasure coursed through my body. I clung to his neck with both arms, while his free hands played alternately with my tits underneath my blouse.

He started thrusting, ramming his dick in slow strokes at first, savoring each penetration, then increasing the tempo as the delicious friction of my pussy slapping against his dick made him hornier all the more. I was stifling my moans of pleasure as he fucked me harder and harder, and faster and faster, the bookshelf was steadfast against the onslaught of lust and passion.

Every thrust wracked my body with exquisite joy that I sucked his tongue and basked in the superb sensations coming from my tits and pussy.

And I had thought he was naïve and inexperienced.

"I'm almost there," I murmured, gasping.

He didn't say anything but he growled and locked his pelvis into mine as he drove deep into my pussy. I clung to him as my climax burst and assailed my body with thousands of needle-prick vibrations. I nibbled his lips as I gyrated my hips against him to savor the indescribable pleasure.

Then he grunted and withdrew his penis, as he massaged his shaft and his semen squirted happily into the floor. We kissed each other passionately, fully satiated with our sexual adventure.

I was prepared for this day, and I cleaned up the mess and wiped all traces from our bodies before we slipped back to our table.

I straightened my hair and gave him my sweetest smile. I knew I was glowing beautifully. He, too, appeared more handsome and sure of himself.

He said it first, "Can we do this again sometime?" I nodded happily.

"Some place more private."

.   .   .

I nodded excitedly and imagined the endless erotic positions, I could do with Al. At last, I would no longer be having imaginary sex, and be masturbating alone.

CHAPTER 7

NAUGHTY NURSE LIZA
MAKES A HOUSE CALL

HI, my name is Liza Conway and I am an experienced RN. I'm a great nurse and I usually spend my working hours at Boston General Hospital, but this week I was filling in for a nurse friend of mine and doing her home health nurse calls. I was always happy to be of service as a nurse in more ways than one! Yes, I freely admit I am horny all the time. I am a blazing nympho. I don't try to hide it or keep it a secret. Anyone who knows me knows I love to fuck and suck any which way but loose.

Today I was scheduled to make a house call on an older gentleman. I would try to control my animal urges, but my weakness has always been for older men. I am thirty years old and as far as I am concerned the older the better! I tapped on the door lightly once I arrived at Mr. Johnson's house. He answered slowly but when he got one look at me his eyes perked up and hopefully his cock did too. I had full intentions of seeing if that happened for sure. He led me inside to his bedroom where his medical stuff was. He was diabetic and had to be monitored closely. I was sure glad to find out if his ticker was in tip-top shape!

I instructed the older man to sit down so I could examine him. I examined him very closely, that's for sure! I had a way with my patients and I feel quite sure they would all say I did. I loved my patients and I also went out of my way to ensure they felt their very best. I did the general check-up of Mr. Johnson and then I accidentally dropped my stethoscope. I bent down to get it making sure I showed my hairy snatch to Mr. Johnson. I knew I had an older male patient today, so I didn't wear any panties of course.

I thought Mr. Johnson might choke when I had my pussy splayed in all her glory right in his older face. From behind, I took my middle finger and ran it around my pronounced clit that now stood out from its hood like a mini cock. I did figure eight circles around the hard clit. Then I plunged my index and middle finger into my snatch hard and yanked them back out again with cum strands hanging from them. I flipped my body around and then one finger at a time I ate the juice off of my horny and greedy fingers. Mr. Johnson naturally plunged his hands underneath his robe. I could see his hand movements stroking ever so slowly under the fabric. That is all it took to send me to my knees and suck his old but hard prick. Seeing a man stroke under his pants always drove my nympho cunt wild!

I sucked like it was the first cock I had sucked in 6 months. I got the entire dick in my mouth and I could reach down with my tongue and tickle his frenulum. I thought he might jump off the edge of the bed when I tickled the fuck out of it. He moaned in complete ecstasy and pushed my dark-haired head down onto his prick harder.

"Suck me harder Nurse Liza. Please suck the fuck out of me!" Mr. Johnson proclaimed. "Toy that nasty bush," he said as I fingered the hell out of my greedy cunt. I was happy to do anything it took to make the old guy feel better than he had in weeks.

"Hop on my dick and screw me, nurse." Without even removing my nurse's dress I hiked it up to my waist. I swung one leg over his body and looked down at my pussy and lowered myself easily down onto his cock that was standing up like a soldier to attention.

"Mmmm you feel so damn good inside my bush," I told Mr. Johnson. I wanted him to feel good so he would provide me with the stiffest boner imaginable. He did just that and then some. I grinded slow and seductively atop his proud prick. He put his aged hands on my ass and helped move it the way he liked upon his swollen cock. This old guy has an incredible dick rim that grazed my g-spot to the point of sexual nirvana. I wanted as much of this dick as I could get and for as long as I could get. As I said I am a dirty nympho. I love sex so much I could literally do it 24/7. Then he took his hands and bounced me on his raging cock. That was a move that I thoroughly enjoyed. I asked him if I could flip around and grind the reverse cowgirl way. "Sure you can baby." He said impatiently.

I turned around and mounted Mr. Johnson on a reverse cowgirl style. He moved my hips seductively round and round in figure eights. He was balls deep inside me and I was bucking him like a wild bronco.

I got to the edge of orgasm and then slowly inch by nasty inch lifted up off of his dick. I knew he was getting a bird's eye view of my swinging pussy lips and my fat bush. Mr. Johnson groaned like a rabid beast and his balls drew up with the wrinkled skin hardening into sexy naughty delight. When he came his cockhead seemed to swell to the size of a plum. All I could feel was it pulsating inside my horny wet cunt. My pussy shivered and then spat back at him with my white-hot cunt juice. My cunt felt like it was on fire, and the thick seed he was pumping into me wasn't putting that fire out. It was only making me hotter. I wanted to taste my cunt on his cock so I pulled it out of me and sucked his nasty ramrod dry Well, time for the rest of my rounds," I said with a smile. "Hope you sleep well tonight."

CHAPTER 8

SEX GAME'S BAIT BITCH

I'M A HOT BLONDE FEMALE. Boys have been all over me since I was sixteen. They didn't all get to fuck me, I just necked and petted and gave blowjobs. So two weeks ago, when I turned eighteen, you'd think I'd go wild and fuck a hundred men. It didn't happen. The computer happened. I surfed around and did Youtube.com and Deviantart.com and other places before I found this AI computer sex game site called "Computer Places Your Mom Never Allowed You to Surf."

A bit of rebellion lingered in my young female blood. Besides, now that fucking might really happen, my horny factor reached off the charts! I clicked on the site. A saucy list of sex games popped up.

A blonde girl wants to lose her virginity to a dirty older man of sixty-three. The young woman can't pay off her drug dealer and decides to sell him sex.

A drug-addicted dad asks his white virgin daughter to fuck a group of African American guys for more drugs.

I selected the third one. Believe me, more harsh selections waited. But I've always wanted to do some interracial fucking. I live out in the country, in Austria. If I see a black man, usually it's because it's night and he is a white man standing in the shadows gawking at my hot young body. So this might be the nearest I'll ever be to giving a black guy my white pussy.

I pressed enter. Suddenly the computer screen showed this dilapidated black neighborhood. I see this strawberry blonde with freckles and two ponytails looking scared. She looks old enough to be eighteen though. Her dear Dad has just dropped her off and one of those black dudes hands him drugs. Three other black guys waiting eyed her young white freckled body up and down, with bone-hard delight.

All of them start talking about her heavy naked DD cup tits pressing against her white sleeveless T-shirt. "Fuck University" splashed across the hills of her tits and the flatness of her belly. Her black Dukes of Hazzard cutoff jeans barely covered her pussy lips between her creamy white legs. She's wearing gym shoes and white socks. They talked about everything the girl wore.

One black guy called her a saucy slut!

. . .

This is where it gets weird. I paused taking in the computer screen scene. Three of the black guys wear gold jewelry. One guy's black baseball cap is screwed on sideways. Another is holding a joint and about to smoke it. The screen reads, "Press Play to BEGIN--If you DARE!"

I've never resisted a dare in my life. I pressed the button and somehow I ended up inside the screen. I look back and clearly see the computerized slutty strawberry blonde girl laughing. She's sitting on my bed in my bedroom looking down at me inside the sex game. "You horny slut. Tricked you again. You're going to be fucked raw!"

Right there I got kind of scared.

"Yeah, what the freckled blonde says is true. I'm afraid," said the black guy, not a hair on his head or face, but wearing the biggest gold medallion. His medallion was big as a dinner plate. "And you're gonna love it!" said the black guy holding the joint. "Want a puff to get you started? Marijuana contains chemicals that relax the pussy muscles."

"I'm going to cum in your asshole, Sweet White Virgin," said the third black guy who had a beard, mustache, and an afro the size that Don Cornelius of Soul Train would envy.
  "I'm just going to lick your pussy till you come," said the yellow-skinned black guy. "I'm the leader." He spoke softly at first then yelled. "Now get your ass on the hood of that car."

. . .

By this time, Dad drove off in his limo after the marijuana guy gave him the drugs.

The sweet leader guy came up to me and deftly unhitched my jeans using one hand. They fell to my ankles. I forgot to wear panties today. I walked butt naked over to an old rusty green

Chevy Nova. The tires were gone and the back windshield cracked. Inside the car looked like an impromptu trash can. I noticed the rusty tan color getting all over my hands. "I'm not getting that on my legs, pussy, or ass. Ewwwe," I squealed.

"Give her your black trench coat Goldie," ordered the leader.

For the life of my tender pussy, I didn't understand why a black guy had a long black trench coat during the peak of summer. Whatever! He laid his trench down on the beat-up Nova. I hopped up and spread my legs for the soft-spoken leader

"Bon cunt appetite!" he said as he moved in to chow down on my blonde bushy pussy.

His lips did a number of moves on my pussy folds; moves that made my inner lips stand up straight, and made my large labia's spread wider apart. I humped against his smooth black face, letting his mustache wash my clit of all her juicy sauces. When he was done, I lay back exhausted. He snapped his finger and it was Goldie's turn.

Goldie, wearing that huge gold plate, pulled me closer to the car's edge until my hot V fit perfectly around the O of his huge black cock. He wasted no time shoving his cranny hunter everywhere to hunt out all my girly juices. I swear he stretched my pussy back at least two inches. Luckily, for me, I rode horses on the farm, or a major blood bath might appear on Goldie's black trench. When he finally froze stiff, He sent his copious black genes to meet my white genes deep inside my labyrinth womb. Now it was the marijuana black dude's turn.

He offered me a hit. I declined. "I want to remember every fuck and thrust and grind and grunt from this sexperience." I smiled my white teeth made the marijuana guy smile too. He fucked me as the marijuana joint hanged precariously out of his lip, dropping ashes on the left side of my hip.

After him, I fucked the last black guy. My womb now sloshed holding three loads of sperm spurts. Then I hoped all their slippery sperm dripping down to my ass crack helped the ass fucking. It did. It hurt a bit at first. But I scooped up all their sperm leaking out of me and rubbed it on his narrow dick and the butt fucking turn out the best of all. When they were done, a big sign came across the sky that read: Hit BEGIN to play again or END to quit."

· · ·

I looked up at the nasty little strawberry ponytailed bitch and said, "If you hit END, I'll make sure you get fucked by the biggest black men the next time I play."

That saucy ponytailed white bitch nodded passively and pressed BEGIN. I ended up on the dilapidated street like before. Only I, and the girl, remembered how the whole thing played out.

CHAPTER 9

TEACHER'S PET

ANGELICA PARKER COULD FEEL the moistness between her thighs. She stared at the unsmiling, 36- year old Math instructor in front of her, and her nipples tingled with excitement. She'd have to get banged today, or she'd get mad with desire.

She crossed her legs trying to appease her hot, pulsating clit that had for months hungered for the professor's dick. God, how she would love to suck him dry and give him a spine-tingling blowjob.

The bell rang and everyone hurried home. It was their last class and it was 7 in the evening so everyone was exhausted and wanted just to go home.

Angelica approached the professor boldly and said:

"Can I talk to you for a minute, sir?"

The handsome professor turned and was startled when Angelica's lips were on his own, hungry and demanding.

He tried to push her aside and started to say something but Angelica's tongue closed in on his lower lips, preventing him from speaking. Her hands shot to his crotch, and he shuddered as her fingers ran up and down his shaft beneath his slacks.

"I know you want me," Angelica hissed into his ears. "You're just trying hard to ignore it," she continued. "Well, I can't. I want you to fuck me hard and long. Fuck my brain out until I beg for mercy."

Ben's erection was instant, evident underneath his slacks, as he breathlessly crashed Angelica towards him. Soon, the school guard would do the rounds, but Ben was beyond caring now.

"That's right Ben, fuck me," Angelica urged him on, placing one of Ben's hand inside her undies.

Ben gasped with desire when his fingers came in contact with her hot, moist pussy. Angelica clambered into the teacher's table to spread her thighs for Ben's hungry tongue. He was onto her in an instant. He shoved his tongue into Angelica's tight vagina and tasted her juices, sighing contentedly as she became moist all the more. He had always dreamt of fucking Angelica but he didn't act on his desire because that could mean his expulsion as a faculty member but tasting the young girl's pussy had made him mad with lust.

He licked and sucked the outer lips of her vagina, and then lapped her clitoris. She moaned, as in pain, and urged him not to stop. It was growing dark but they didn't bother to turn on the lights. He sucked and licked her clitoris repeatedly until she started to meow like a kitten.

Ben stopped and pulled his pants down to direct Angelica into his throbbing, angry phallus. She went down on the floor and grasped his penis with her fingers while massaging them steadily. Ben raised his head as in supplication and groaned. "That's it, yeah," he urged her.

Angelica licked the tiny opening of his dick and then ran her tongue around his crown, as he grasped a handful of her hair to prod her to take him into her mouth.

"Be patient," she crooned, as she ran her tongue tantalizingly, up and down his manhood.

When she sensed he was ready, she took him into her mouth and started bobbing in and out. Ben was groaning pleasurably, while he stood, with his pants down, and she was kneeling, her other hand fondling her pussy.

Suddenly, a door banged in the corridor; the janitor was doing his rounds.

With their faces suffused with lust, Ben and Angelica scrambled to the last row, where the long table hid them from plain sight.

Ben lay on the floor as Angelica continued pleasuring him beyond what he had ever imagined. The janitor took a peek inside the room and closed the door shut. Now, they had all night fucking their brains out.

"I can't submit my assignment tomorrow now, sir," Angelica stopped her ministrations. "Oh god, I don't care about assignments," he hissed, "please continue what you're doing."

Angelica smiled and stooped again to suck his enormous, red dick into her mouth. He was hyperventilating and clearly ready to explode.

She mounted him then, planting her palms on his sinewy chest. She guided her rock-hard penis into her warm, tight pussy and moaned in delight as every nook in her pussy was filled with his enormous dick. When she started moving up and down, he groaned and grabbed her ass to pound his dick relentlessly into her moist pussy.

They were both moaning wildly, as their groins met and skin slapped against the skin. She added more sensations to her building orgasm, as she gyrated her pubis and clitoris against Ben's to stimulate her clit.

Ben reached out to grasp her tits and tweak her nipples, she bent down to suck his lower lip as their arousal continued to smolder and blaze.

He stopped with a grunt, pushed her, and propped her on the table. He had always imagined fucking her on the table. She was completely naked now, and she was a beautiful sight to behold, with her young and proud nipples enticing him to fondle them.

Angelica smiled impishly and spread her thighs wide as he shoved his delicious dick into her eager, dripping pussy. "Ahh, that feels good," she crooned. She kissed him full in the mouth and they kissed and sucked each other's tongue as he continued going in and out of her in his standing position. He basked in her tightness and aggressiveness. The sensations caused by her tight pussy were exquisite, Ben thought, "I'm ready to die."

His hand played with her tits now and then, tweaking her clit when he withdrew. Angelica felt her orgasm coming. "I'm coming," she cried in delight. "Fuck me harder."

Ben went crazy with lust as he felt his climax on its threshold too. He rammed his dick harder, going in and out of her tight pussy, relishing the incredible sensations, he thought she would never experience. Angelica was writhing in pleasure as she climaxed and rotated her hips round and round as she savored his dick. She made unintelligible noises as she climaxed again and again.

This drove Ben in frenzy, he went faster and harder thrusting with all his might until he shuddered with incredible delight. Then he withdrew his dick and massaged it. His semen squirted between Angelica's breasts as she knelt to nuzzle his dick and take it into her mouth.

They collapsed on the bare floor and embraced each other, exhausted but satiated. Ben had his arm underneath Angelica's head.

"Let's do that again," Ben said and touched Angelica's face.

"With pleasure, sir," Angelica teased him, "Let's do it over and over."

CHAPTER 10

THE NAUGHTY NANNY

MY NAME IS Natasha and I am a nanny for all of the rich kids that live in my upper-class neighborhood. I enjoy taking care of the little rug rats and I especially love it when I got to take care of their daddies too if you know what I mean.

This particular day I was off to work at Robinson's house. This was one of my very favorite nanny gigs because I happen to love sucking Mr. Robinson's big dick off. He always called me to babysit when he knew his snooty wife was going to be gone away on business.

I got to the sprawling two-story dream house about 5 minutes early. As I thought, Mr. Robinson answered the door. "Hello, Natasha," he said in a very business-like manner, but he wasn't fooling me. Once you got this old guy behind closed doors, he became a tiger in bed. He was part of a married duo that was the older of the pair and he possessed a young wife who was obviously only interested in the dude's cash flow.

It became really apparent once he and I began fooling

around. This cat was horny all the time. I don't think his wife ever gave up her pussy for him. He practically chased me around the bed the first time I came over to his home. He was bound and determined to get laid and there wasn't anything I could do to stop him, and I really didn't want to. I found out that day that older men are the best in bed by far. Younger men don't near hold a candle to the things an older dick can do with his cock and any cunt he can happen to get his greedy hands on.

I went about my babysitting and got the children off to bed around 9 pm. I was kind of surprised their dad hadn't said anything to me. Oh well, I bet he will be ravaging my horny body in a few moments. He always did love devouring my luscious long lipped pussy. I lightly tapped on Mr. Robinson's door to inform him the children were all snug in their beds. He opened up the door and much to my surprise he stood there wanking his long hard prick until he was bright pink and swollen. I dropped to my knees and kicked the door shut behind me and started to nurse his older dick for all it was worth.

By the way, he had to hold on to the bureau for support, I could tell the fucker liked me sucking his balls deep. I was the type of nanny that truly liked being a caretaker for everyone in the family. While I was sucking the dick, he handed me a paddle. He liked me to paddle his white ass while I performed a bj on him. He said, "Spank my ass harder, Natasha, make my cheeks pink." I paddled him a bit harder while he yanked my bulbous nipples out and applied nipple clamps to them. I sucked him like a vacuum cleaner while he twisted the clamps harder upon my nipples.

I knew it was time I get this dude over to the bed before h-e hyperventilated on me. Even though he was at least 67 years old, he had quite a bit of spunk left in him. I liked getting on top of his older dick and rubbing my clit all over his silver cock bush. He would take his false teeth out too and let me tell you he could flat eat some pussy and suck my nipples real damn good toothless. In fact, I'd venture to say that Mr. Robinson ate my bush out better than any man or woman ever had. It worked well if I squatted over his gray head and his aging face so if he needed air I could simply lift my cunt up about 3 inches above his head with my horny lips dangling. Sometimes I'd even engage Grandpa Moses in a game of catch my lips if you can. I really couldn't understand why his trophy wife wouldn't let him bang her. He was playful trying to grab my cunt lips in his mouth; his prick was skinny but hard as steel and he made a feast out of cunt.

I rode him slow and gentle and writhed my hips over his hard cock and bush until I reached near orgasm. I suddenly sat straight up on him, threw my head backward, and gritted my teeth. I knew I had a good orgasm coming soon. Before I knew he was doing it, I felt his gray-haired balls draw up and press into my anus. I knew then he was shooting hard. After he shot off like 5 wads, he was always ready to wallow in my snatch. He sat down with his face right in my cunt, held my legs out to his sides, and then quickly threw his face down in it and began eating with all of his might. I yelped like a puppy as he tickled my clit head with his tongue tip.

"Fuck fuck...that feels good," I exclaimed in a fevered and horny voice.

.   .   .

I took my hands and pressed the old guy's face harder and deeper into my seething love box. I could see him wanking his dick off again with his right hand while he wallowed down in my thicket of hairy lust and cream.

ABOUT THE AUTHOR

Kenna Divens is an emerging erotica author of many erotica kinks and sub-genres. Be sure to check out other books and leave a review if this story got you hot!

Visit my blog at Kenna Divens Blog

Join my newsletter for exclusive Kenna Divens Newsletter

Sign up for Free Stories from Xplicit Press Authors

Xplicit Press Author Updates

Like Xplicit Press on Facebook

Follow Xplicit Press on Twitter

Readers: I want to expand a few of the stories to see where the characters can be explored further. If there are any of the stories that you would like to read more about again, I'd love to hear from you!

Keep In Touch
Kenna Divens
info@kennadivens.com